IMPROVE YOUR MEMORY SKILLS

Struan Reid

Edited by Corinne Stockley
Consultant: Maggie Hilton
Designed by Brian Robertson
Illustrations by Paddy Mounter

Additiona Lyon

Contents

American edition 1988.

First published in 1988 by Usborne Publishing Ltd, 20 Garrick Street, London WC2E 9BJ, England. Copyright © 1988 Usborne Publishing Ltd.

About this book

Do you forget things throughout the day, things that you want to remember? Are you bad at remembering people's names and faces, telephone numbers and addresses, a lesson at school or a simple shopping list?

Psychologists generally agree that it is possible to improve our memory skills, but also that this cannot be done overnight, without commitment and memory training. What this book does is to lead you through just such a course of training aimed at improving your methods of remembering things. It explains a series of memory systems that should help you to absorb information in such a way as to recall it more efficiently.

But this book also tries to improve your memory in an enjoyable way, so that the hard work does not become too difficult.

Pages 4-9 give a brief introduction to the human brain, how scientists think our memories work and why we forget things. On pages 10-11 there are some simple tests to see how good your memory is at the moment.

Pages 12-15 list various useful tips and suggestions that will help prepare you for the memory systems that follow.

On pages 16-31 you will find the various memory systems that are designed to help you to develop a more efficient memory for all sorts of things. They begin with the simple systems and then gradually become more sophisticated.

Towards the end of the book, in the black-and-white section, you will find a series of tests on the various memory systems explained in the color section. These should show you how much your memory has improved since you first started reading the book.

On pages 42-46 there is a useful section on preparing yourself for exams, a check-list that should help to make you more confident.

What is memory?

Memory is the ability to store and recall information. Scientists believe that things we experience with our senses, (sight, sound, touch, smell and taste), are stored in our brains and nervous systems in the form of permanent chemical changes.

All learning is based on memory. Memory enables you to read this book. Ordinary, everyday things, such as walking, are based on memory. Without memory we would react to every situation we encountered as if we had never experienced it before.

The control centre

The central nervous system is the body's control centre. It is made up of the brain and spinal cord, both of which contain millions of nerve cells known as neurons. These transmit and receive the electrochemical "messages" (nervous impulses) which are responsible for all our physical and mental activities. Memory is just one of the mental activities, just as thinking is another.

Brain box

The human brain contains about one million, million neurons. They are so small that more than 20,000 could fit on top of a pinhead.

Fast impulses

The nervous impulses travelling to and from the brain can move as fast as racing cars. The fastest recorded travelled at nearly 290 km/h (180 mph).

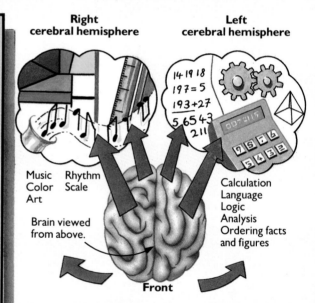

Right cerebral hemisphere

Left cerebral hemisphere

Music
Color
Art

Rhythm
Scale

Brain viewed from above.

Calculation
Language
Logic
Analysis
Ordering facts
and figures

Front

Our personal computer

The largest area of the brain, with many deep folds in it, is called the cerebrum. The cerebrum is made up of two cerebral hemispheres. Broadly, the two hemispheres deal with different mental operations. The left side of the brain deals mainly with calculation, language, logic, analysis and ordering facts and figures. The right side of the brain deals mainly with music, rhythm, color, scale and art.

How the brain remembers

Scientists are unsure exactly how memories are stored in the brain, but there have been a number of theories.

An early idea

The first important theory on memory, known as the Wax Tablet Hypothesis, was introduced by a Greek philosopher called Plato in the 4th century BC. He believed that the mind is like a block of wax and that impressions are made on it in the same way that wax can be marked with a pointed stick. The impressions, or memories, stayed until they were gradually worn away.

◀ If mice were trained in this exercise...

...they would ▶ forget it when given the drug!

Chemical explanation

A more recent theory is based on the chemistry of the brain. Scientists have discovered that a substance in the body known as RNA (ribonucleic acid) makes proteins (found in all living things). A lot of activity in the brain, such as learning and memorizing, is accompanied by an increase in the amount of RNA and a change in its chemical structure. A number of experiments have been carried out to test this theory. In one experiment, mice were trained to perform a particular exercise. They forgot the exercise when they were given a drug which stopped the production of RNA.

Localization

The localization theory suggests that memories are stored in particular areas of the brain, such as those called the temporal lobes.

Dispersed memory

Another view holds that memories are not stored in a particular area of the brain, but over the whole of the brain. Each part may contain our experiences.

Memory stored in particular areas of the brain.

Memory stored all over the brain.

How your memory works

We rely on our memories to help us through each day. The pieces of information that we use are stored in our memories like information in a filing cabinet. But the information needs to be well-organized so that it can be easily retrieved for later use.

Three stages of memory

Scientists today think that the memory goes through three stages: immediate memory, short-term memory and long-term memory. Some people also refer to the "three Rs" of memory: registration, retention and retrieval.

1 Registration of information

2 Temporary retention of information

3 Permanent retention of information

1. Immediate memory is also known as "sensory memory". It holds information coming in from the senses for very brief periods, less than a second, before the information is either rejected or passed on to the short-term memory store.

2. Short-term memory can hold about seven items at one time. Information it holds is easily disturbed and if it is not rehearsed immediately it will be forgotten within about thirty seconds. Short-term memory is used when we want to hold information temporarily, for example a telephone number or figures in mental arithmetic. While something is in short-term memory, parts of it are being selected to go into long-term memory and the rest is being rejected, i.e. forgotten. Short-term memory is like the "in tray" of the brain.

3. Long-term memory is the filing cabinet of the brain. It can store any number of pieces of information and can last for a lifetime. Some psychologists divide long-term memory into two kinds: episodic and semantic. Episodic memory consists of remembering incidents, such as childhood recollections or a film you saw. Semantic memory consists of remembering knowledge about the world, for example the name of a mountain or city or the meaning of words.

Immediate memory — Senses register and compare information

Information in

Short-term memory — Temporary retention of information

Long-term memory — Permanent retention of information

Retrieval of information for use

Rejection of information

The senses and memory

Many things can call up memories for people. Sounds, smells, tastes, sights, particular places and moods can all conjure up memories of past events. There are different types of memory related to the senses, for example olfactory (smell), tactile (touch), emotional (feeling), kinesthetic (physical movement). But most people remember better things they have heard or seen.

Which are you best at?

Think about what you had for breakfast this morning. Can you smell all the items again? This is an olfactory memory.

What did the cereal box, milk jug or jam jar feel like in your hand? This is a tactile memory.

If you went out after breakfast, can you remember the route you took? Were there trees or houses or both at the sides of the road? This is a visual memory.

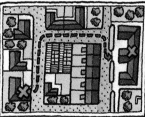

Can you remember turning a handle to open a door, or did you just push it open? This is a kinesthetic memory.

Can you remember the conversations you may have had during the day? This is a verbal memory.

How were you feeling at different times in the day? Happy? Sad? Nervous or excited perhaps? This is an emotional memory.

Auditory memory

If you have a good auditory memory you will be able to remember things you hear, such as a tune or language, better than things you see. You will learn better by listening or reading out loud.

Blah . . .

Blah . . .

Visual memory

A good visual memory means that you are best at remembering things you see, such as the layout of a room or the details of a picture. You will learn better by reading, i.e. seeing words.

Why do we forget?

People often say that they have a "good memory" or a "bad memory", but things are not as simple as that. Different people are better at remembering different things. For instance, you may be very good at remembering telephone numbers but quickly forget tunes or faces. In order to understand memory, we also have to understand why we forget things. Here you will find out the main causes of forgetting.

Poor registration

If something is to stay in the memory it must be firmly impressed there. In other words it must be strongly registered. We sometimes think we have forgotten something when in fact we never really learned it in the first place.

What's his name?

What's his name?

Poor registration is usually due to a lack of attention. When someone says: "I can't remember that person's name", it often means that no attention was given to the name in the first place. Lack of attention may in turn be caused by a number of things, such as lack of interest or concentration on other matters.

Repression

There is also a way of subconsciously forgetting painful memories, known as "repression". For example, if someone wants to believe they are doing very well at school, the fact that they are doing badly at a particular subject may be forgotten, buried low down in the memory store.

Disuse

Even if information is properly registered and stored, it may still be forgotten because of disuse – that is, it is rarely retrieved and used. This is the brain's way of clearing out "junk". So if you want to remember facts you have learned, you must revise them regularly.

Concentrating on other things

Emotional problems are some of the most common causes of students failing their exams. They cannot pay attention to their studies because they are concentrating on their personal problems. Love, anxiety and depression are all very powerful emotions that can make it difficult to concentrate on other matters.

Interference

Learning something new can interfere with the memories of material learned earlier on. This is known as "retroactive inhibition". Studies have shown that, after a break, students could remember 56% of material they had learned, but only 26% if they had learned something new between the first learning and testing.

There is much more interference between two similar subjects than between two unlike subjects. The memory of a French lesson would not be upset too much if it was followed by a chemistry lesson. But the interference would be much greater if it was followed by something similar, such as a German lesson.

Another form of interference through learning is known as "proactive inhibition". This is when what has been learned before interferes with what is being learned now. Again, similar subjects interfere more, such as learning one poem and then another poem.

Haven't a cue

Another theory on why we forget is that the right cue to locate the information is missing. You may have the information stored away in your memory but be unable to get at it. This is a bit like trying to find a book in a library without knowing the author's name.

Remembering people can be made difficult by the way in which they change their appearance, for example their clothes and hair. In other words, the familiar cues have been changed. A change of location can also be confusing. You may see Petronella Biggs every day in one situation, but pass her in the street without recognizing her.

It's me!

Another example is when you have a piece of information on the "tip of the tongue". You know you know it, but it stays just out of reach, either until you find the right cue or until it is given to you by somebody else.

Trying out your memory now

Although you may think that you are very forgetful, it is actually very surprising just how many things you can remember. You can identify thousands of objects, places and people, as well as knowing a number of facts about each one. You can also remember facts about many more things you may never have seen, such as deserts, dinosaurs and historical battles. This book will help you to improve your ability to add to this list.

Test yourself

These two pages contain some basic memory tests. Take a piece of paper and a pen, and try them all now. This will give you an idea of how good your memory is at the moment, before you read about the various ways you can improve it.

Names to faces

Look at the ten faces and names shown here for two minutes and then, using a piece of card or paper, cover up the names and try to match the right name to the right face. Score out of 10.

Mr Schmidt

Mrs Westbrook

Mrs Wong

Mr Rogers

Miss Pouget

Mr Blacker

Mrs Roberts

Mr de Souza

Mr Olaf

Mr Brown

Long numbers

3786414937

7263418975

9267891182

5946388421

5832418235

Look at the five ten-digit numbers listed here, one after the other, giving not more than about 30 seconds for each one.

Now cover the numbers and try to write each one down on a piece of paper. Score one point for every digit that you manage to place in its proper sequence. Score out of 50.

378⟨46⟩14937   7263418975✓   9463⟨33⟩31

Numbers and items

In just two minutes, try and remember the various items that are listed here with their numbers.

Write down each of the items beside their correct number in the following order: 15, 9, 10, 3, 4, 18, 13, 7, 2, 6, 11, 19, 8, 5, 1, 12, 14, 20, 16, 17. Mark yourself out of a score of 20.

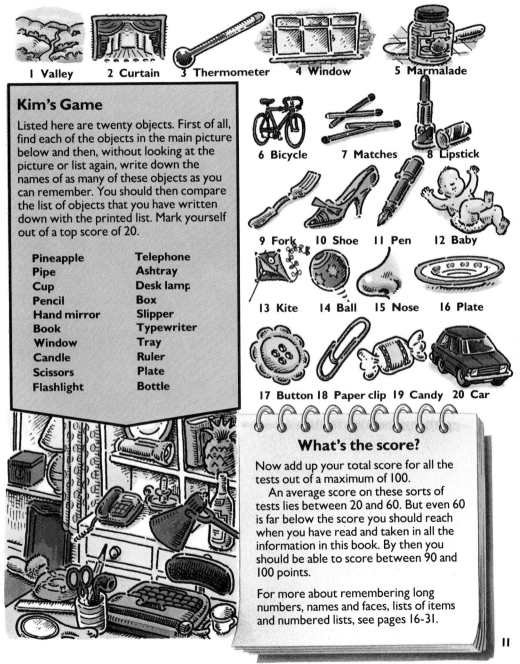

1 Valley   2 Curtain   3 Thermometer   4 Window   5 Marmalade

6 Bicycle   7 Matches   8 Lipstick

9 Fork   10 Shoe   11 Pen   12 Baby

13 Kite   14 Ball   15 Nose   16 Plate

17 Button   18 Paper clip   19 Candy   20 Car

Kim's Game

Listed here are twenty objects. First of all, find each of the objects in the main picture below and then, without looking at the picture or list again, write down the names of as many of these objects as you can remember. You should then compare the list of objects that you have written down with the printed list. Mark yourself out of a top score of 20.

Pineapple	Telephone
Pipe	Ashtray
Cup	Desk lamp
Pencil	Box
Hand mirror	Slipper
Book	Typewriter
Window	Tray
Candle	Ruler
Scissors	Plate
Flashlight	Bottle

What's the score?

Now add up your total score for all the tests out of a maximum of 100.

An average score on these sorts of tests lies between 20 and 60. But even 60 is far below the score you should reach when you have read and taken in all the information in this book. By then you should be able to score between 90 and 100 points.

For more about remembering long numbers, names and faces, lists of items and numbered lists, see pages 16-31.

Basic memory rules and tricks

You should always try and stick to certain basic rules of memory, whether you are trying to remember everyday things such as appointments or telephone numbers or whether you are trying to remember a lot of more complex material, perhaps for exams. Some of the basic rules listed below are expanded on pages 42-46, which is a section on revision techniques for exams.

Try to be interested

It helps a great deal in remembering things if you are interested in what you are trying to remember. It is difficult to learn anything in which you are not interested and more difficult to retain it.

Understand it

Learning something means understanding it. You cannot remember what you have never known. If you do not understand the material, ask someone to explain it to you and then read through it again.

Confidence counts

People who think they have poor memories often do have poor memories because they lack the confidence to remember. They should think: "I can remember and I will remember".

Paying attention

In order to remember something you must learn it and in order to learn it you have to pay attention to it. For example, reading is more than just looking at words: you also need to think about what the words are saying. Learning is impossible when the attention is wandering.

Overlearn it

The more thoroughly something is learned, the longer it is remembered. Get into the habit of frequently revising material you have learned. Even when you think you have memorized a fact, go on repeating it for a little longer.

Rehearsal

Material is learned more quickly if you rehearse it to yourself or out loud at frequent intervals while you are trying to remember it. This makes you pay more attention to the material. It makes you use your ears, which are almost as much a help in learning as your eyes.

Some extra help

Here are some simple tricks for dealing with the problems of everyday remembering. They should only be used as extra "back-up" and you should try not to get into the habit of using them instead of your memory.

In your way

If you have to take something with you when you leave home in the morning, place it in front of your bedroom door or the front door.

Bands and pins

Anything unusual will act as a reminder of something you should do. Try putting a rubber band round your wrist, or pinning a safety pin to your bag.

Notices

Write yourself a big note and stick it somewhere where you will see it, on the bathroom mirror or the front door.

A poetic memory

A psychologist called E. Titchener learned Milton's poem "On the Morning of Christ's Nativity" (244 lines long) when he was eight years old. He could still recite the poem when he was sixty.

Odd positions

If an important thought passes through your mind when you drift off to sleep, tip the shade on your bedside lamp to a sharp angle. Or throw a pillow across the bedroom where you will have to step on it. In the morning you will see what you have done and the memory will gradually fall into place.

Habit

You can remember something you should do by relating it to something else that has become a habit. For example, if you have to take pills at night, attach the pill bottle to your toothbrush in some way. When you clean your teeth you will remember to take the pills.

Changing your watch

If you wear a watch, a good trick for remembering something is to change it over to the other wrist. When you next want to check the time, a bare wrist will trigger the memory of what it is you have to do.

Preparing yourself

We all spend a lot of time sorting through the information we encounter every day of our lives. The ability to organize the information and to compare and associate it with other information are keys to a good memory. The various memory systems all rely on organizing, associating and visualizing techniques.

Organizing

A good memory is like a well-organized filing system. Information stored in an organized way is rarely forgotten. If a new fact presents itself, you first have to decide whether to keep it or not. If you decide to keep it, the next problem is where to place it. Organizing things into groups is essential to remembering them. The organization can be divided in the following three main ways.

Sequencing

This involves arranging things in series, such as 1-2-3-4, A-B-C-D and Spring-Summer-Autumn-Winter. You could not find a book in a library or a telephone number in the directory without sequencing. (Library books are usually arranged alphabetically.)

Categorizing

This means putting things into groups of similar things. Supposing you had to learn the following words: kettle, daffodil, sofa, bowl, rose, stool, plate, armchair and crocus. It would be easier to remember them under the following group headings decided by their function:

Kitchenware	Flowers
Kettle	Daffodil
Bowl	Rose
Plate	Crocus

Furniture

Sofa
Stool
Armchair

Red with red

Another form of categorizing involves linking things that are visually similar. For example, square things with other square things and red things with other red things.

Square with square

Associating

The more a fact can be associated with other facts, the better it will be remembered. You can remember where Madagascar is by associating it with Africa. When you connect two things in your mind, you do so because they have something in common.

For example, you may walk past a red bicycle in the street and suddenly remember that you have to return a book to a friend of yours. The two things are not directly connected, but are associated in your mind because your friend owns a red bicycle.

Visual images

You should try to think of mental images connected to the thing you want to remember in order to strengthen the memory of it. The more you can visualize, the quicker your memory will improve. Visual images are some of the most useful memory joggers. You will find them a great help in using the various memory systems that follow in this book.

The visual images that you think up can be more easily recalled if you stick to the following basic memory rules.

1. Exaggeration. Make important details in your images larger than life, such as size or quantity. For example, you may want to remember to take your tennis racket out with you. Imagine it taking up the whole length of your hallway at home.

2. Contraction. Similarly, making an object much smaller than usual can be helpful. You could then imagine a tiny tennis racket hanging from the front door handle.

3. Make the image as unusual and ridiculous as possible. If you wanted to remember to go and feed the goldfish before a music lesson, you could visualize a giant goldfish playing a violin or piano.

4. Use lots of color in your image. The more color there is, the stronger the image will be. So your goldfish should be a very brilliant gold color.

5. Get your image moving in some way. The more movement, the better. Imagine the fish playing the violin fast and furiously.

6. Use all your senses when thinking up the image: taste, touch, vision, sound and smell. You could hear the sound of the violin and even the tune. Perhaps you could see the sheet of music. You could smell the fish and feel the slipperiness of its scales.

The Link System

This is the most basic of all the memory systems and will give you a foundation on which to build the more advanced systems. It involves forming a vivid visual image of each item in a list to be learned and then linking these images together. The second image is linked up with the first, the third with the second and so on, until all the items are linked in pairs. In thinking up the images, you should follow the tips on visualizing that are explained on page 15.

When to use the Link System

The Link System is useful for memorizing lists such as a shopping list or a list of things to take on vacation or do before you leave.

It is also useful for memorizing notes for an exam. This is done by pulling out a key word from each main point of the notes and then linking these words together using your vivid visual images. The key words act as memory joggers.

You will also find further uses of this system with speeches, articles, scripts and jokes on pages 20-21.

Thinking and linking

You may have a list of twenty points that you wish to make in a geography essay.

Thinking of the points carefully, try and form a vivid mental image for each one.

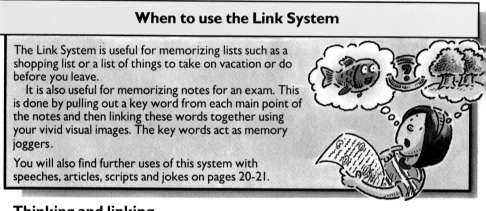

China   Oil   Pagoda

A Chinese bowl

Suppose the first item in your list is "China". Close your eyes and try and create a vivid and striking image of a porcelain bowl. Do not just see the word "China", but actually see a brightly colored bowl.

Slipping along

You must now link, or associate, China to the next item in your list, which may be "oil". The association must be as absurd as possible. For example, you could imagine the bowl walking along until it steps in a pool of oil, slips and flies up into the air.

Now forget about the bowl and link the oil to the next item, possibly "pagoda". Carry on like this until the end of the list.

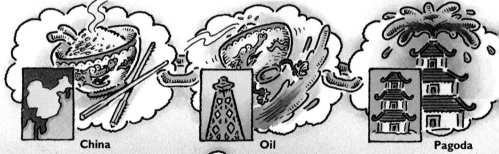

When you have linked all the items, put away your list and see if you can write down the main points of your essay in the right order. As you recall the linking words, you should also be able to remember what you wanted to say about each one. If you have forgotten any words, try to strengthen their images (see page 15).

Put them in the picture

If you find it difficult to remember the first point in the list, try linking it to the teacher who teaches the subject. For example, you could try and see the teacher wearing a bowl as a hat.

The story method

In this variation of the Link System, the items to be remembered are woven into a story. You begin with the first item and then proceed through the story, picking out the key words as you meet them. But with this method, the longer the list, the harder it is to include each item into an easy story.

You may have a list of the following five items you want to pack for your vacation: shirt, trousers, book, hat and toothbrush. You could make up a small story in the following way: the trousers put on the shirt and walked out to the bookshop. He bought a book and then went off to have lunch with the hat and toothbrush.

You can find more tests on the Link System on pages 34-35.

Top score

A German conductor called Hans von Bülow read once through a symphony that he did not know and then conducted it that same evening without the help of the score.

The Room System

This method of memorizing is probably the oldest memory system. It is thought to have been devised more than 2,400 years ago by a Greek poet called Simonides. The system involves choosing places or areas as locations which are known as loci (loci is the plural of locus, the Latin word for place or location). The things to remember are then linked up in a mental image with the chosen loci.

When to use the Room System

The Room System, like the Link System, (see pages 16-17), is useful for memorizing lists, such as the main points in a lesson, various jobs you have to do or shopping you must buy.

You will find further uses of this system over the page with speeches, scripts and jokes.

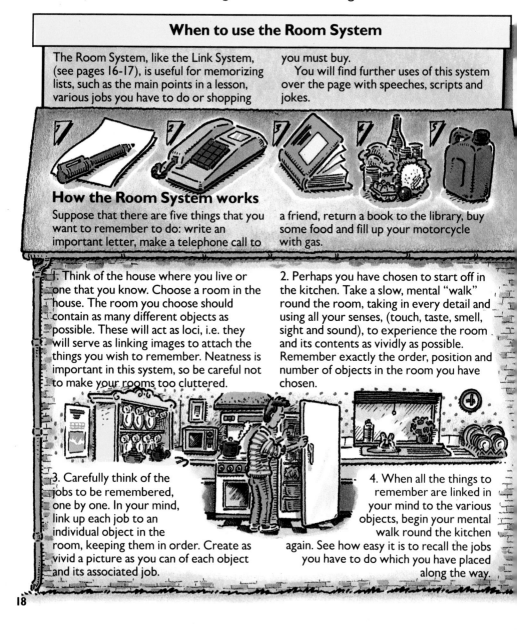

How the Room System works

Suppose that there are five things that you want to remember to do: write an important letter, make a telephone call to a friend, return a book to the library, buy some food and fill up your motorcycle with gas.

1. Think of the house where you live or one that you know. Choose a room in the house. The room you choose should contain as many different objects as possible. These will act as loci, i.e. they will serve as linking images to attach the things you wish to remember. Neatness is important in this system, so be careful not to make your rooms too cluttered.

2. Perhaps you have chosen to start off in the kitchen. Take a slow, mental "walk" round the room, taking in every detail and using all your senses, (touch, taste, smell, sight and sound), to experience the room and its contents as vividly as possible. Remember exactly the order, position and number of objects in the room you have chosen.

3. Carefully think of the jobs to be remembered, one by one. In your mind, link up each job to an individual object in the room, keeping them in order. Create as vivid a picture as you can of each object and its associated job.

4. When all the things to remember are linked in your mind to the various objects, begin your mental walk round the kitchen again. See how easy it is to recall the jobs you have to do which you have placed along the way.

Setting the scene

Object: Kitchen table
Job: Write a letter.
Image: Think of the kitchen table covered with a giant letter acting as a tablecloth.

Object: Toaster
Job: Return book to library.
Image: Imagine the book in the toaster, popping up like a piece of toast, with the title clearly written on the colorful cover.

Object: Sink
Job: Fill motorcycle with gas.
Image: Think of the shiny faucets on the kitchen sink pouring out smelly gas instead of water.

Object: Washing machine
Job: Make telephone call.
Image: Put a bright red telephone in the washing machine. You can hear the gurgling ringing tones through the water.

Object: Oven
Job: Buy some food.
Image: Imagine the food, perhaps a pie, in the oven. You can smell the delicious cooking smells and see the pie crust browning.

A way with words

A Roman philosopher and statesman called Seneca is said to have been able to memorize and repeat 2,000 words after hearing them just once.

Using more rooms

If you have a long list of things to remember, group them in different rooms of the house. This makes it easier to remember them. You can even use parts of the garden.

Now turn to page 35, where you will be tested on a list of things to do.

Speeches, scripts and jokes

The Link and Room Systems described on the previous pages can be applied to many different things you need to memorize. For instance, they will be useful for remembering the main points of a speech or talk you have to give in front of an audience, for remembering scripts from plays, for poems and for jokes.

Talks and speeches

It makes it much easier to deliver a speech if you realize that in most cases you do not need to memorize the speech word for word, just as long as you get all the main points over. In any case, word for word memorization often means that you will end up sounding stilted and wooden and your audience will lose interest .

The secret of giving a good speech is to write down and remember a series of key words that will trigger the main points of the message you want to put across.

First of all, write out and read the entire speech. When you are satisfied with it, read it over once or twice more to get the gist of it.

Try reading it out loud to an imaginary audience, to find out how it sounds and if there are any alterations that you should make.

Now, on a piece of paper, write down in the order they appear a list of key words that summarize the main points you wish to make in the speech.

Trying it out

You could keep the list of key words in front of you as you give the speech, but if you have mastered the Link and Room Systems you could use them to keep the points in your head and so dispose of the list altogether.

Suppose you have to give a talk about plants and animals from all over the world. Your list of key words may include the following: ferns, butterfly, oak tree, monkeys, Amazon jungle and rhododendron.

Using the Link System, you should then link, in vivid mental images, ferns to butterfly, butterfly to oak tree, oak tree to monkeys and so on. Each key word should remind you of the point you have to make, right to the end.

Poems and scripts

It is usual to learn poems and scripts from plays word for word. But the trick for memorizing in these cases is not to learn the material line by line, but to read through the complete poem or script from beginning to end, several times a day over a number of days.

After about the twentieth reading you will be able to recall, without looking at the text, most of the material to be remembered from the poem or script.

You can now apply the key word system to fix the poem or script in your mind. Select as many key words as you feel you need and link them together. Then test yourself by reciting from memory the section of script you are working on and then checking it for accuracy.

Jokes and stories

Your memory in this area will improve right away if you use the Link System.

Just take a few key words from the joke or story, (one from the beginning, one from the middle and one from the punch line), that bring the entire joke or story to mind. You should then link up the key words to make the story.

Carrying cards

Putting key words on cards that you can carry around with you and read in spare moments will also help you to fix speeches, scripts and jokes in your mind.

6,666 in 6

In 1967, Mehmed Ali Halici of Ankara, Turkey recited 6,666 verses of the Koran from memory in six hours.

Remembering faces and names

Faces and names are some of the most important things to remember, but they can also be the most difficult. The problem of fitting a name to a face is not easy because the face is something seen while the name is something heard, two different senses. Most of us are "visualizers" (see page 7), that is we find it easier to remember what we have seen rather than what we have heard. So the trick is to form stronger visual images, as described on page 15, and then consciously link these to the name in some way.

Face-watching

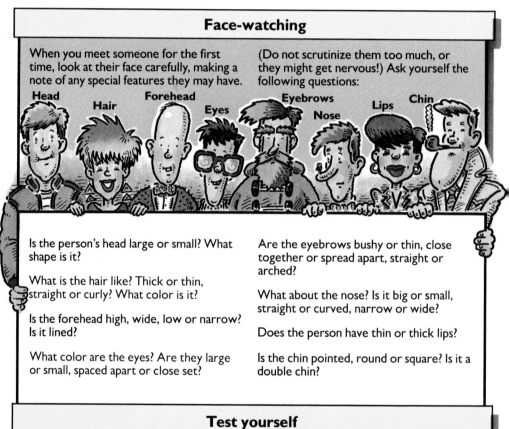

When you meet someone for the first time, look at their face carefully, making a note of any special features they may have. (Do not scrutinize them too much, or they might get nervous!) Ask yourself the following questions:

Head **Hair** **Forehead** **Eyes** **Eyebrows** **Nose** **Lips** **Chin**

Is the person's head large or small? What shape is it?

What is the hair like? Thick or thin, straight or curly? What color is it?

Is the forehead high, wide, low or narrow? Is it lined?

What color are the eyes? Are they large or small, spaced apart or close set?

Are the eyebrows bushy or thin, close together or spread apart, straight or arched?

What about the nose? Is it big or small, straight or curved, narrow or wide?

Does the person have thin or thick lips?

Is the chin pointed, round or square? Is it a double chin?

Test yourself

You could test how keen your observation is already by trying to describe to one of your friends another person that you both know. Work through the features listed above and see how long it takes for your friend to realize who it is you are describing.

Catch that name

When you are being introduced to someone, try and pay as much attention as you can to the sound of their name. This is just as important as familiarizing yourself with their face.

Even if you have heard the person's name clearly, ask the owner to repeat it and even to spell it out to you. The more it is repeated, the more firmly it will become implanted in your memory.

My name is...

Putting names to faces

All names can be divided into two main groups: names that mean something to you, (such as Brown, Long and Page), and names that have no meaning to you.

With the names that do have some meaning, try and link up the name to the person in some way. Sometimes the name does suggest the person: Mr Short may well be short and Mrs Baker may well have soft, white skin like a baker's dough. Sometimes the name may suggest a completely opposite type. It may be easy to remember Mr Short if he is very tall.

Mr. Short   Mrs. Baker

With the names that have no obvious meaning, you must use your imagination to invent one. Think of a noun that sounds as much like the name as possible and form a vivid visual image linking the noun to the name. For example, a Mr Unwin could be pictured as an onion.

Mr. Unwin

If no noun suggests itself, pick out the most prominent feature of the person's face, maybe bushy eyebrows or small lips. Whatever it is, form an exaggerated image of it and then associate your image with the name of the person. You could imagine someone with very bushy eyebrows as having hedges on his forehead.

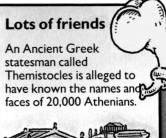

Lots of friends

An Ancient Greek statesman called Themistocles is alleged to have known the names and faces of 20,000 Athenians.

Close encounters

Look closely at the twelve faces shown below and try to memorize the names, using the techniques described on pages 22-23. Then cover the names and see how many faces you can name. You could also try describing the faces to a friend, who must see if they can give you the right name.

1 Mrs Frankfurt

2 Mr Singh

3 Mr Wright

4 Mrs Fouquet

5 Mrs Holmes

6 Mr Spright

7 Miss Killjoy

8 Mr Evans

9 Miss Leigh

10 Mrs Osakwe

11 Mr Mendonza

12 Mr van Arpt

Page 37 has a further test, where the same faces and names are in different order.

The Peg System

There are three main versions of the Peg System: the number-shape version described below, and the alphabet and number-rhyme versions over the page. They use a set of "peg words" (names of objects) to replace a sequence of numbers or letters. The peg words can be used over and over again to remember new items, just as you might use one peg on which to hang many different coats.

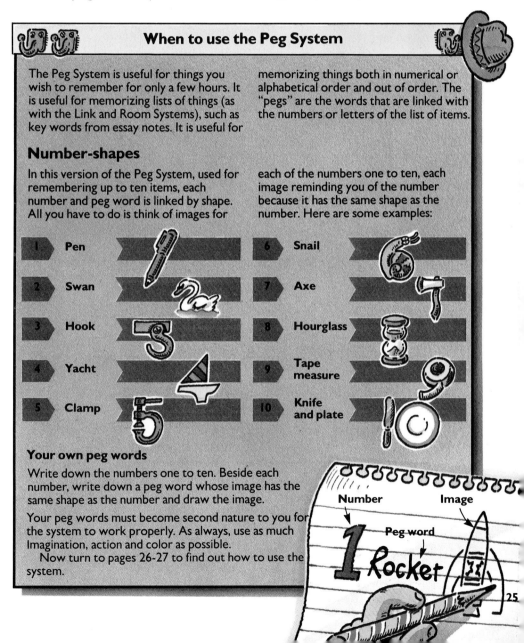

When to use the Peg System

The Peg System is useful for things you wish to remember for only a few hours. It is useful for memorizing lists of things (as with the Link and Room Systems), such as key words from essay notes. It is useful for memorizing things both in numerical or alphabetical order and out of order. The "pegs" are the words that are linked with the numbers or letters of the list of items.

Number-shapes

In this version of the Peg System, used for remembering up to ten items, each number and peg word is linked by shape. All you have to do is think of images for each of the numbers one to ten, each image reminding you of the number because it has the same shape as the number. Here are some examples:

1	Pen		6	Snail
2	Swan		7	Axe
3	Hook		8	Hourglass
4	Yacht		9	Tape measure
5	Clamp		10	Knife and plate

Your own peg words

Write down the numbers one to ten. Beside each number, write down a peg word whose image has the same shape as the number and draw the image.

Your peg words must become second nature to you for the system to work properly. As always, use as much Imagination, action and color as possible.

Now turn to pages 26-27 to find out how to use the system.

Number   Image

Peg word

1 Rocket

Using number-shapes

Supposing you have to remember up to ten things you need to do in the evening. The first item might be: "Write an essay about Julius Caesar". You could use the number-shape method in the following way.

The number-shape for 1 could be "Pen". You could link 1 with Caesar by thinking up a vivid image of Caesar going into battle waving a pen instead of a sword.

Test yourself

For each of the ten things on your list, think up a visual link with your peg word for its number on the list. Then take three pieces of paper and write down the numbers one to ten, first in the correct order, then in reverse order and finally in random order.

Now cover your list of things to remember, and try to fill out each of the three numbered lists by recalling which item you hung on each peg word. Cover up each list as you finish it. Try testing yourself again later to see how many items you remember.

List in order

1	6
2	7
3	8
4	9
5	10

List in reverse order

6	5
7	4
8	3
	2
	1

List in random order

6	10
2	8
9	5
4	7
1	3

Number-rhymes

In this version of the Peg System, also used for remembering up to ten items, the peg words chosen rhyme with the numbers they represent. Here is a list of rhyming peg words for the numbers one to ten.

1 - Bun
2 - Shoe
3 - Tree
4 - Door
5 - Hive
6 - Sticks
7 - Heaven
8 - Gate
9 - Wine
10 - Hen

An epic feat

A British historian called Lord Macaulay could recite all of Milton's poem "Paradise Lost" (12 books long) without a single mistake.

The alphabet method

The alphabet method is the last type of Peg System. It works in a similar way to the number-shape method, but where this is used with numbers and can really only be used for ten items at a time, the alphabet method uses the 26 letters of the alphabet and so allows you to remember up to 26 items at a time.

How it works

The peg words chosen must begin with the sound of the letters they represent, if this is possible. Otherwise they must simply begin with the letter, (as with H, W and Z below). They must also be easily memorized. For example, for the letter A you could choose from, among others, "Aviator", "Ace" and "Ale", all beginning with the sound "ay".

If the letter itself makes a word, (for example, "C" makes the sound "sea"), then that should be the word used. This should help you to remember the peg word.

Here is a list of possible peg words that can be used in the alphabet method.

	Peg word
A	Aviator, Ace, Ale
B	Bee
C	Sea
D	Deer, Deal
E	Eel
F	Effluent, Effigy
G	Jeans
H	Hat
I	Eye
J	Jay
K	Cake, Cape
L	Elephant
M	Embassy, Emperor
N	Enemy, Envelope
O	Oasis, Opal
P	Pea
Q	Queue
R	Ark, Art
S	Essay
T	Tea
U	Ewe
V	Venus
W	Watch
X	X-ray, Exercise
Y	Wine, Wire
Z	Zebra

Make your own list

As in the other methods, choose your own peg words, as they will mean more to you than someone else's. Use as much imagination, action and color as possible when picturing your peg words, so that when you later come to use them, you can form vivid visual images with the things you want to remember.

On a piece of paper list in a column the letters A-Z. Beside each letter write in your choice of peg word.

Beside each peg word, draw a picture of the peg word. By doing this you will be strengthening the image even more in your mind.

Remember your peg words

You can test yourself by opening up a book and calling up the image of each peg word with each letter in a sentence. Do this until all 26 images come quickly to mind.

The Number-Consonant System

This is the most sophisticated and versatile of all the memory systems. Although it requires a great deal of effort to master, it will pay large dividends. It will show you how to count with objects instead of numbers. It acts as a giant filing system with which you can remember any amount of verbal or numerical information.

Learn the alphabet

In order to learn the Number-Consonant System, you must first learn a simple phonetic alphabet, in which each of the numbers from 0 to 9 is represented by one or more consonant sounds. The system is based on this alphabet becoming second nature.

The phonetic alphabet

Number	Sounds
0	z, s
1	d, t, th
2	n
3	m
4	r
5	l
6	j, dg, sh, soft ch, soft g
7	k, hard c, hard g
8	f, v, ph
9	p, b

How it works

Once the alphabet is learned, numbers of any length can be replaced by words. These are formed by combining the consonant sounds with vowels. Words are easier to remember than numbers.

With this system you can turn numbers into nonsense syllables, words or phrases. For example, the number 314,094 can become "motor zebra" in the following way: 314 094
mtr zbr

314   094
mtr z br

mtr zbr

o o ← vowels → e a
motor zebra

In the same way 59,410,215 becomes "leopard sandal":
5941 0215
lprd sndl

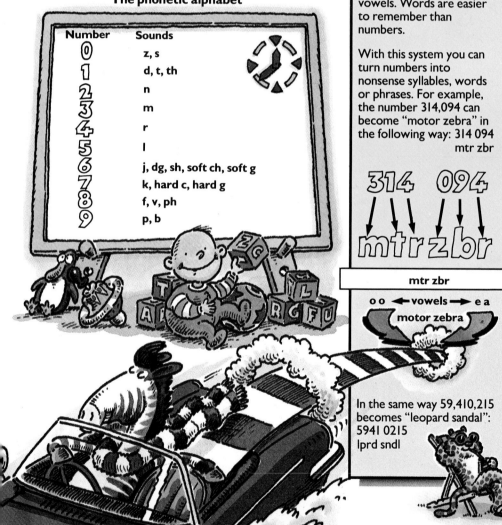

You must first learn by heart the sounds representing each digit so that you can bring them to mind in any order and form words from any number.

Ask a friend to call out random words or numbers and see if you can answer with the correct numbers or suitable words derived from the phonetic alphabet.

With practice, you will find that long numbers will be much easier for you to remember. You can find more tests with long numbers on page 40.

Going further

Now you know how the Number-Consonant System works. Over the page you can find different uses for it.

The system can also be used to extend your list of peg words (see pages 25-27).

For example, here is a list of suggestions for the numbers 11-20.

11	Tot, teeth
12	Tin, tan, dune
13	Tomb, dam
14	Tire
15	Towel, tail, doll
16	Dish, tissue
17	Tack, duck, deck
18	Dove, toffee
19	Tub, tube, tap
20	Nose, knees

Even bigger numbers

The system can be expanded up to 50, 100, 1,000 or even higher numbers. But do not be tempted to expand your list until you have completely mastered the numbers 11 to 20.

On a piece of paper, list the numbers 10 to 20. Beside each number write down your own choice of peg words (you can use your number-shape peg words for the numbers 1 to 9 – see page 25). Now write a list of 20 things you may have to do over a given weekend, and try to form a visual image to "hang" each item on its peg.

Now cover both lists and see how many of the items you can remember. You could get a friend to test you by calling out the numbers in random order.

29

Using the Number-Consonant System

For long numbers

The Number-Consonant System is very useful for remembering strings of numbers.

Suppose you had to remember the number 352951941725. You could break the number down into more manageable groups of digits with their words. Thus, 352=mln=melon; 951=plt=pilot; 941=prt=pirate; 725=cnl=canal.

In order to remember the original long number, all you have to do now is to use the Link System (see pages 16-17), weaving the words together with imaginative links.

For example, you could imagine melons being dropped by a pilot on a pirate ship travelling along a canal.

Shapely numbers

If you get the order of the words muddled up, you can solve this by using the number-shape method (see page 25) instead of the Link System.

Using the original number at the beginning again, 352951941725, you would simply link "melon" to your number-shape image for 1 ("pen"); "pilot" to the number-shape image for 2 ("swan"); "pirate" to your number-shape image for 3 ("hook") and "canal" to your number-shape image for 4 ("yacht").

So you could picture the melon stabbed through with a pen, swans dressed in pilots' clothes, pirates brandishing hooks and finally, the canal filled with hundreds of yachts.

Try it yourself

Go through your address book and write down a list of telephone numbers that you would like to remember. Translate them into words or phrases. Try and connect the person you want to remember to the number in a vivid visual image.

For history dates

To remember history dates, you change the last three digits of the date into a word. (If the date has four digits, the first digit is unnecessary as it is usually a "1". For dates in the 20th century you can use just the last two digits.) The words can then be linked visually with the events.

For example, in order to remember the date of the outbreak of the Second World War, 1939, you can drop the first digit, 1, to leave just the last three, 939. These translate into the consonants "pmp" which easily translate into "pump".
  You could imagine a soldier spraying water from a water pump.

Suppose you had to write an essay about the entry of Britain, Denmark and Ireland into the EEC. The Paris Summit in October 1972 was a meeting to decide about it, and the countries finally joined in January 1973. You could remember this by showing the flags of the three countries being carried in a canoe (72 = cn) towards a giant comb entry gate (73 = cm).

For appointments

For this system, every day of the week is represented by a number as follows: Sunday 1, Monday 2, Tuesday 3, Wednesday 4, Thursday 5, Friday 6, Saturday 7.
  A day has 24 hours, from 24 (midnight) through 1 (1am), 12 (noon), 13 (1pm) and back to midnight. So for any hour and day of the week you can form a 2 or 3-digit number, the day first and the hour second.

You can then translate the number into a word and link the word with a vivid visual image to an appointment you have on that date.
  For example, you may have to catch a very early flight on Wednesday (fourth day of the week) at 1am. This translates to 41.
  You need to form an image between "rd"/"radio", the peg word for 41, and airplane. You could imagine a radio with wings and tail flying round your room like an airplane.

For tests on appointments and history dates, turn to pages 40-41.

Mnemonics

Mnemonics, or memory aids, are named after Mnemosyne, the Greek goddess of memory. Each one is an individual memory jogger for a particular fact. A mnemonic can be simple or complicated, sensible or silly. Sometimes the sillier it is the better. Some of the more common ones are listed here. But they are just a few examples. Perhaps you know many more.

Rhyming mnemonics

Because material with rhythm is easier to remember than material without rhythm, before the invention of writing most information was memorized in the form of rhymes. These were further strengthened with music and dancing. Below are some well-known, more recent, rhyming mnemonics.

Thirty days hath
September, April, June and
November. All the rest
have thirty one, excepting
February alone, which has
but twenty eight days clear
and twenty nine on each
Leap Year.

I before e
except after c,
or when sounded like a,
as in neighbor or weigh.

In sixteen hundred and
sixty-six
London burned to a pile of
sticks.

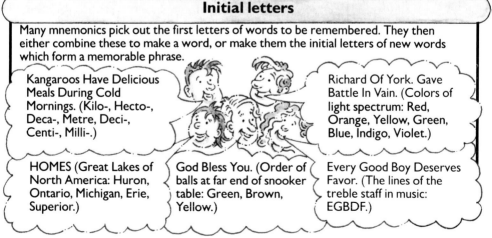

In fourteen hundred and
ninety two,
Columbus sailed the ocean
blue.

When the face is red,
raise the head.
When the face is pale,
raise the tail.

Right over left,
then left over right,
and you can pull a
square-knot tight.

Initial letters

Many mnemonics pick out the first letters of words to be remembered. They then either combine these to make a word, or make them the initial letters of new words which form a memorable phrase.

Kangaroos Have Delicious Meals During Cold Mornings. (Kilo-, Hecto-, Deca-, Metre, Deci-, Centi-, Milli-.)

Richard Of York. Gave Battle In Vain. (Colors of light spectrum: Red, Orange, Yellow, Green, Blue, Indigo, Violet.)

HOMES (Great Lakes of North America: Huron, Ontario, Michigan, Erie, Superior.)

God Bless You. (Order of balls at far end of snooker table: Green, Brown, Yellow.)

Every Good Boy Deserves Favor. (The lines of the treble staff in music: EGBDF.)

Thinking up your own mnemonics

You can make up your own rhyming mnemonics or initial letter mnemonics to help you remember facts or lists of items. Remember these following points:

Rhyming mnemonics work particularly well when numbers are involved:
598-2266
is the number of Polly Hicks.

A new word, maybe a made-up nonsense word, from initial letters is easier when there are vowels:

KHRANX (The noble gases: Krypton, Helium, Radon, Argon, Neon, Xenon.)

Mnemonics using initial letters for new words, and a phrase, work well when there are no vowels:

Farmers Plant Turnips For The Market Pigs. (Bones of human leg and foot: Femur, Patella, Tibia, Fibula, Tarsals, Metatarsals, Phalanges.)

Simple alphabetical lists of initial letters are also useful when there are no vowels:

BBMMP (Shopping list: Bread, Butter, Milk, Meat, Potatoes.)

Test yourself

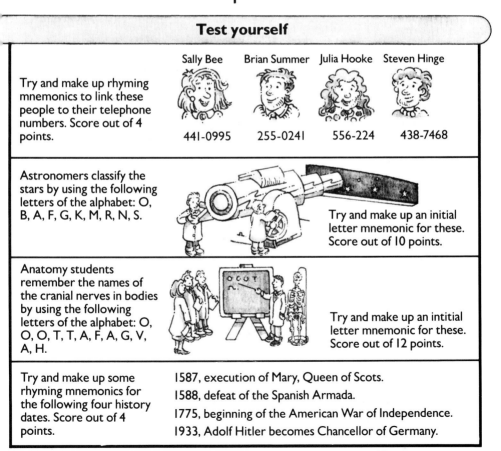

Try and make up rhyming mnemonics to link these people to their telephone numbers. Score out of 4 points.

Sally Bee	Brian Summer	Julia Hooke	Steven Hinge
441-0995	255-0241	556-224	438-7468

Astronomers classify the stars by using the following letters of the alphabet: O, B, A, F, G, K, M, R, N, S.

Try and make up an initial letter mnemonic for these. Score out of 10 points.

Anatomy students remember the names of the cranial nerves in bodies by using the following letters of the alphabet: O, O, O, T, T, A, F, A, G, V, A, H.

Try and make up an intitial letter mnemonic for these. Score out of 12 points.

Try and make up some rhyming mnemonics for the following four history dates. Score out of 4 points.

1587, execution of Mary, Queen of Scots.

1588, defeat of the Spanish Armada.

1775, beginning of the American War of Independence.

1933, Adolf Hitler becomes Chancellor of Germany.

You can find suggested answers to these tests on page 47.

Tests on the memory systems

On the following eight pages you will find various tests that will show you how many of the memory systems you have managed to master. Whereas at the beginning of the book a good score for the tests would have been about 50%, you should now be near a top score of about 100%. Work out your score at the end.

Test yourself on the Link System

Remember that the entire Link System, described on pages 16-17, requires associating the first item to the second, the second to the third, the third to the fourth and so on. It is very important to see associated images of the items in your mind's eye. But each mental association need be seen for just the smallest fraction of a second, before going on to the next item.

Here is a list of forty random items. Using the Link System, see both how many of the items you can remember and how many you can remember in their correct order. Read slowly through the list once only. Now, without looking at the list again, write down the items one by one in their correct order. Once you have done that, check your list with the original.

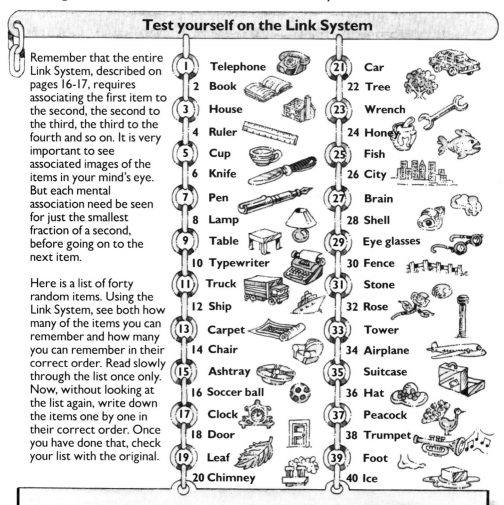

1	Telephone	21	Car
2	Book	22	Tree
3	House	23	Wrench
4	Ruler	24	Honey
5	Cup	25	Fish
6	Knife	26	City
7	Pen	27	Brain
8	Lamp	28	Shell
9	Table	29	Eye glasses
10	Typewriter	30	Fence
11	Truck	31	Stone
12	Ship	32	Rose
13	Carpet	33	Tower
14	Chair	34	Airplane
15	Ashtray	35	Suitcase
16	Soccer ball	36	Hat
17	Clock	37	Peacock
18	Door	38	Trumpet
19	Leaf	39	Foot
20	Chimney	40	Ice

You should score in two ways: first score out of 40 for the number of items you remembered and then score out of a further 40 for the number of items you listed in their correct order (note that if you reversed two items, they are both wrong with regard to order). The top possible score for this test is therefore 80 points. If you find that you have forgotten a large number of items, try strengthening your mental images, using the techniques described on page 15.

Test yourself with the story method

Using the story method variation of the Link System, described on page 17, see how many of the following ten jobs you can remember.

Score in the same way as on page 34: first add up the number of jobs you remembered out of 10 and then the number you remembered in their correct order. (Again, if you reversed two of the jobs, they are both wrong with regard to order.) The total possible score is 20 points.

Carefully look at the various jobs below and then weave them in order into a connected story.

1 Feed the cat

2 Make a telephone call

3 Write your diary

4 Clean your bedroom

5 Write a letter

6 Wash your hair

7 Pump up your bicycle tires

8 Look for your train ticket

9 Buy a book

10 Pack your suitcase

Test yourself on the Room System

Imagine you have five further jobs to do on another day, listed below. Carefully look at the five things to do for just one minute and then, using the Room System described on pages 18-19, see how many of the five you can remember and in their correct order.

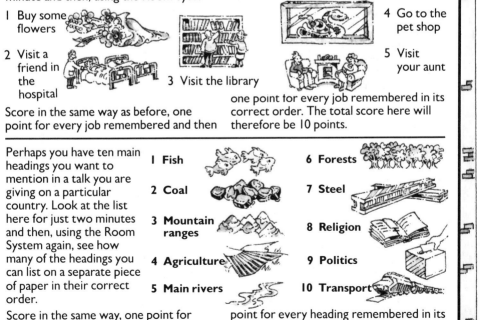

1 Buy some flowers

2 Visit a friend in the hospital

3 Visit the library

4 Go to the pet shop

5 Visit your aunt

Score in the same way as before, one point for every job remembered and then one point for every job remembered in its correct order. The total score here will therefore be 10 points.

Perhaps you have ten main headings you want to mention in a talk you are giving on a particular country. Look at the list here for just two minutes and then, using the Room System again, see how many of the headings you can list on a separate piece of paper in their correct order.

1 Fish

2 Coal

3 Mountain ranges

4 Agriculture

5 Main rivers

6 Forests

7 Steel

8 Religion

9 Politics

10 Transport

Score in the same way, one point for every heading remembered and then one point for every heading remembered in its correct order. Score out of 20 points.

Test yourself on speeches and articles

Here is a short speech that someone may give when accepting a sports trophy on behalf of their team.

First of all, I would like to say that this is the first speech I've ever made, so you'll have to forgive me if I sound nervous! I hasten to add that this is not the first trophy the team has ever won, but our gallant captain, who usually accepts such honors, is ill with the 'flu. I'm sure I speak for all of us when I say thank goodness he didn't get it until after the final!

I'd like to say a big thank you to our trainer, Angus Macpherson, and to all the people who turned out to support us, despite the horrible weather. For the benefit of those of you who didn't make it, let me just say that it was a thrilling match, and ask you to give three cheers to the unlucky losers.

Look at this speech for no more than five minutes, deciding which are the main points that are being made, and choosing a key word for each of those points.

Now, without looking at the speech again, write down the list of key words that you have chosen.

In front of a friend, see if you can recite the general outline of this speech as if you were standing in front of a large audience.

You can either keep the list of key words you have made in front of you or, even better, use the Link System to jog your memory on each of the main points in order, so you can do without the list.

If you have kept the list of key words in front of you during your recital, your friend can award you a score out of 30 points. But if you have recited the speech without the list of key words to help you, you can be awarded a score out of 50 points.

Impress your friends

Get a copy of today's newspaper or a magazine. Using the Room System, (see pages 18-19), you are going to memorize one item from each of the first 20 pages (just the main headline, i.e. what an article is about or what an advertisement is for).

Go through the pages slowly, picking out one thing to remember from each one. Then choose a room in your house and link each of the 20 items to an object in the room.

Now ask your friends to call out random page numbers from 1 to 20, and impress them by knowing what is on each page.

For your own purposes, score out of 20 points for every item remembered. Score out of a further 20 points for every item remembered in its correct order. The top score possible is 40 points.

Names and faces

Here are the same twelve faces you met on page 24, but in a different order and without their names.

Without referring back to page 24, see how many of the faces you can fit with their correct names.

Write down the numbers as they appear here on a piece of paper and beside them write down the names.

Score one point for every name you fit to its correct face. The top score is a possible 12 points.

Tests on the Peg System

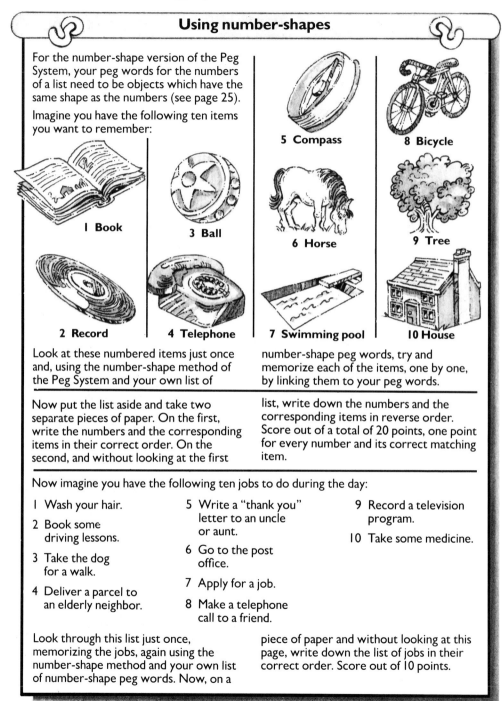

For the number-shape version of the Peg System, your peg words for the numbers of a list need to be objects which have the same shape as the numbers (see page 25).

Imagine you have the following ten items you want to remember:

1 Book

2 Record

3 Ball

4 Telephone

5 Compass

6 Horse

7 Swimming pool

8 Bicycle

9 Tree

10 House

Look at these numbered items just once and, using the number-shape method of the Peg System and your own list of number-shape peg words, try and memorize each of the items, one by one, by linking them to your peg words.

Now put the list aside and take two separate pieces of paper. On the first, write the numbers and the corresponding items in their correct order. On the second, and without looking at the first list, write down the numbers and the corresponding items in reverse order. Score out of a total of 20 points, one point for every number and its correct matching item.

Now imagine you have the following ten jobs to do during the day:

1 Wash your hair.

2 Book some driving lessons.

3 Take the dog for a walk.

4 Deliver a parcel to an elderly neighbor.

5 Write a "thank you" letter to an uncle or aunt.

6 Go to the post office.

7 Apply for a job.

8 Make a telephone call to a friend.

9 Record a television program.

10 Take some medicine.

Look through this list just once, memorizing the jobs, again using the number-shape method and your own list of number-shape peg words. Now, on a piece of paper and without looking at this page, write down the list of jobs in their correct order. Score out of 10 points.

Using the alphabet method

The alphabet method is described on page 27. You use it by linking the item you want to remember to your peg word for the letter representing its place in the list. For example, if your peg word for A is "ace" and the first thing you want to remember is "cat", you could imagine a playing card ace with a picture of a cat on it.

Here is a list of twenty random items to memorize.

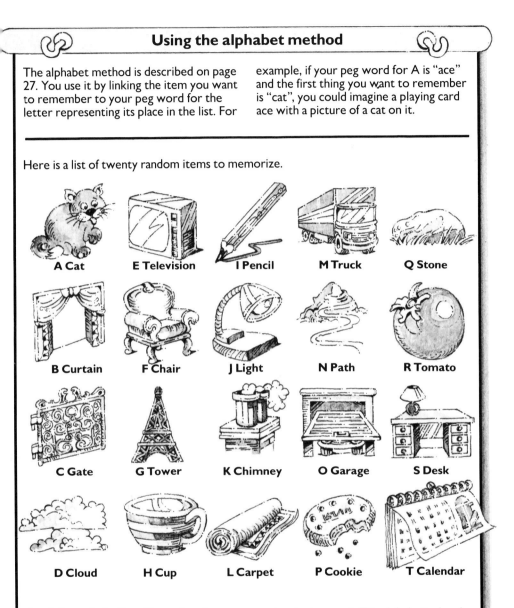

A Cat	**E Television**	**I Pencil**	**M Truck**	**Q Stone**
B Curtain	**F Chair**	**J Light**	**N Path**	**R Tomato**
C Gate	**G Tower**	**K Chimney**	**O Garage**	**S Desk**
D Cloud	**H Cup**	**L Carpet**	**P Cookie**	**T Calendar**

Read through the list of items for about three minutes and, using the alphabet version of the Peg System described on page 27 and your own list of alphabet peg words, try and memorize the items in order. Now put the list aside and take two separate sheets of paper. On the first, write the letters A-T in alphabetical order with their corresponding items. On the second, write the same letters and their items but in reverse order. When you finish the first sheet, put it aside so that you cannot see it when you are filling in the next one. Score out of 40 points.

Tests on the Number-Consonant System

Long numbers

Suppose you have to memorize the ten long numbers on the right.

Using the Number-Consonant System on pages 28-31, try to memorize each of these long strings of numbers, giving not more than 30 seconds to each. Break each up into more manageable groups of three or four digits, changing the digits into letters from your phonetic alphabet (which you should now know by heart) and then forming words from these letters. Then weave the words together as imaginatively as possible with vivid visual images.

Score out of a possible 100 points, one point for every digit remembered in its correct sequence. There are suggested linking words on page 47, to use if you get stuck.

853714999
185946094
352701762
416957016
972940641
6488094532
79941714539
82847455188
60143212195
744115824991

Appointments

Imagine that you have made the following eight appointments, all of which are very important – it is best to memorize them in case you lose your diary.

Monday at 8pm. You have been invited to a friend's birthday party.

Tuesday at 10am. Geography exam.

Tuesday at 2pm. Meeting with your music teacher.

Wednesday at 9am. Appointment with the dentist for a check-up.

Thursday at 4pm. Your parents are celebrating their wedding anniversary.

Friday at 2pm. You have a French test.

Saturday at 8pm. Catch a flight to go on vacation.

Sunday at 10am. You have been invited out on a picnic.

Using the system as described on page 31, give yourself five minutes to memorize this timetable. Then, without looking at this page again, write down the timetable in the correct order. Score one point for each day and time and one for the appointment. Top score of 16 points. There are suggested linking words on page 47, to use if you get stuck.

Amaze your friends

The following method, sometimes referred to as the First Sunday Method, will enable you to know the day of the week for any date in any year you want.

1. For any year, write down the date of first Sunday for each month. For example, for 1988: 376315374264.

2. Memorize these numbers by combining them in twos or threes to make up words from the Number-Consonant System. For example, 37=mac, 63=jam, 15=tile, and so on. The words can then be combined into a story to help you remember.

3. With this number you can name the day of the week for any date in 1988. For example, if you wanted to know the day of the week for the 28th May 1988, first find the fifth digit (representing May), which is "1". So you know the first Sunday in May will be the 1st May. Then add sevens to this figure, so the second Sunday will be on the 8th, the third on the 22nd, the fifth on the 29th. Therefore the 28th May must fall on a Saturday.

Write down and memorize the 12-digit number for any year and get a friend to ask you questions about it.

For example, what date is the 3rd Thursday in May? How many Fridays are there in April? What day of the week did 30th June fall on?

Historical dates

In just three minutes, try to memorize these ten historical dates, using the method described on page 31. Score out of 10 points. There are suggested linking words on page 47, to use if you get stuck.

1725 Death of Peter the Great
1971 Decimalization of British currency
1485 Battle of Bosworth
AD79 Destruction of Pompeii
1492 Voyage of Christopher Columbus

1547 Start of reign of Edward VI
1984 Assassination of Indira Gandhi
1649 Execution of Charles I
1917 Russian Revolution
1914 Outbreak of First World War

Countdown to exams

On the next five pages you will find a series of learning steps, techniques and hints that will take you through from lessons to exams. They suggest how you should approach your work in order to build up your confidence before entering an exam.

Taking notes in lessons

Notes are a written record of a lesson or lecture which can be used for learning and then revision. They help you to remember the main ideas and the important details of a book or course. Make sure you include everything of importance.

There are two main ways of making notes. One is to write a summary of a lesson or lecture with simple sentences, using short, easy words as much as possible and abbreviations.

The other method is to break up the information into its main points, again using simple, abbreviated sentences, and then number or letter these as a list.

Capital letters, underlining, stars and arrows, drawings and diagrams all help to make notes easier to learn.

Be interested

You will learn subjects you are interested in far more easily than those you are not (see page 12). You will not do your best work unless you are interested. So try to develop an interest in all parts of a course.

Try and find connections between new subjects and earlier studies. If you are interested in a subject, it may start an interest in a new one.

Active learning

Make your learning active. Participate in the class by listening, making notes and asking questions. A good teacher should always encourage questions in a lesson.

When you are reading through something, think of the questions the information raises and try and answer them yourself by relating them to other information that you already know.

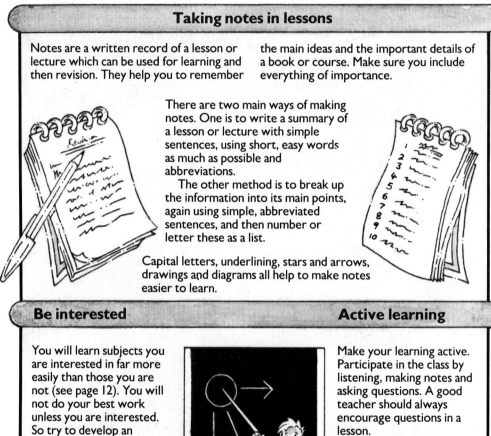

Preparing for revision

Remember the old saying: "A healthy body makes a healthy mind". When you have a period of concentrated study, it is very important to pay attention to looking after your health, eating the right foods and getting enough exercise.

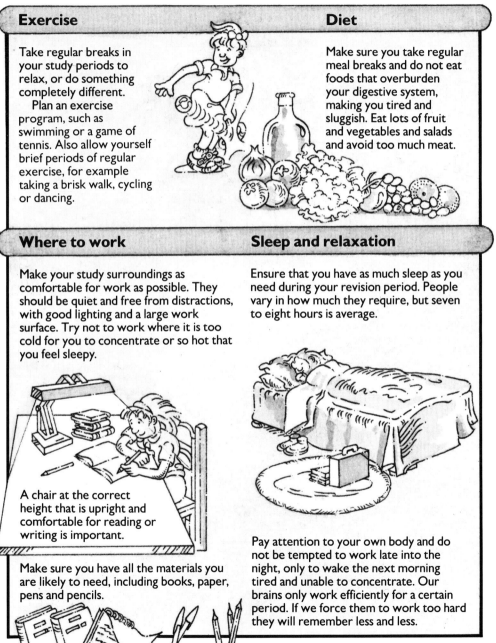

Exercise

Take regular breaks in your study periods to relax, or do something completely different.

Plan an exercise program, such as swimming or a game of tennis. Also allow yourself brief periods of regular exercise, for example taking a brisk walk, cycling or dancing.

Diet

Make sure you take regular meal breaks and do not eat foods that overburden your digestive system, making you tired and sluggish. Eat lots of fruit and vegetables and salads and avoid too much meat.

Where to work

Make your study surroundings as comfortable for work as possible. They should be quiet and free from distractions, with good lighting and a large work surface. Try not to work where it is too cold for you to concentrate or so hot that you feel sleepy.

A chair at the correct height that is upright and comfortable for reading or writing is important.

Make sure you have all the materials you are likely to need, including books, paper, pens and pencils.

Sleep and relaxation

Ensure that you have as much sleep as you need during your revision period. People vary in how much they require, but seven to eight hours is average.

Pay attention to your own body and do not be tempted to work late into the night, only to wake the next morning tired and unable to concentrate. Our brains only work efficiently for a certain period. If we force them to work too hard they will remember less and less.

Planning your revision

If you want to study well you must try to be organized. Find out at what times of the day you learn best. For example, if you work better in the morning, save the more difficult parts of your revision for that time of day.

If you study better in the evening, go to bed after you have finished instead of doing some more work.

Try and revise the material again in the morning, before your other activities during the day make you forget it. You will remember more of the material if you revise it as soon as possible after learning it. This is because the material is quickly forgotten during the first hour after learning it (see page 8).

Try and space out your revision by studying a little at a time. It is better to study regularly for short periods than for one long period. Study periods of about forty to fifty minutes followed by short breaks for rest are usually more efficient.

Study different subjects during the day, so that you stay interested and the subjects do not interfere with each other. For example, do not study two languages together (see page 9).

Try not to spend more time on the subjects you are best at or more interested in so that the subjects you are not very good at receive less attention. If necessary, spend more time on the subjects you are not very good at.

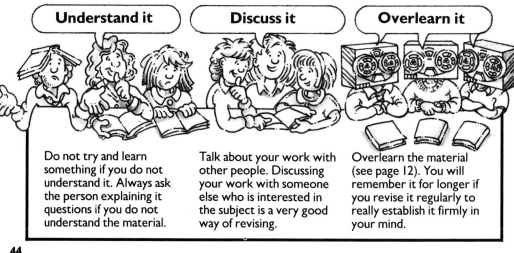

Understand it

Do not try and learn something if you do not understand it. Always ask the person explaining it questions if you do not understand the material.

Discuss it

Talk about your work with other people. Discussing your work with someone else who is interested in the subject is a very good way of revising.

Overlearn it

Overlearn the material (see page 12). You will remember it for longer if you revise it regularly to really establish it firmly in your mind.

Active revision

If you are trying to learn some notes you made from a lesson, make a list of the main points in the notes, one by one. Then put this list away and try to remember the points in order. Try and write down the same list from memory and check this new list against the first. Repeat this until you have remembered all the points.

This is known as active revision and the more you use it, the more you will be made to think and therefore learn during your revision.

At the exam

Make sure you have all the equipment you may need before going into an exam. Always take more than one pen, just in case the first one dries up on you.

Always make sure that you have a watch with you, and that it shows the correct time. You may not be able to see a clock to check how long you have left.

Positive thinking

"This is a slight hiccup, but it is not going to set me back."

Negative thinking

"This is terrible. I am going to fail."

Think positive

It is important to feel confident as you go into an exam in order for you to do your best. No one is expecting more from you than your best. If you do not think positively you might start turning small problems into big ones. Therefore, try and turn any negative thoughts into positive ones.

Reading through the paper

When you receive the exam paper, spend some time reading through it carefully. Do not read it so quickly that you miss the exact instructions.

Check whether any of the questions are compulsory or whether each answer should begin on a separate sheet. If you are asked to give a simple explanation, do not explain in great detail.

Mark the questions that you think you are able to answer. (You could also draw up a reserve list of alternative questions.) Keep away from any questions that are unclear to you.

Do not try to answer more or less questions than asked for or you will spoil your results.

Divide the number of questions to be answered by the time available and set yourself a time limit for each answer. Do not spend too much time on any one question. Leave a little time at the end for rereading the paper and your answers – you may be able to correct some obvious mistakes that you might have made.

Make sure that you understand exactly what the questions are asking, picking out the key words in each. On a piece of paper, or in your head, draw up a list of the main points you want to include in your answers and arrange them in order. Begin a new paragraph for each main point.

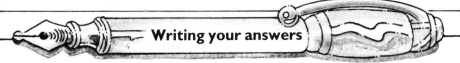

Writing your answers

Long-windedness will put the examiner off, so try to present your answers as clearly and concisely as possible. Make sure that what you write down answers the question as closely as possible and make sure that you cannot be misunderstood.

The examiner will probably not know you and so will judge you by your answers alone. It is important to remember that poor handwriting, spelling, punctuation and grammar will all make a bad impression and may lose you marks.

If you run short of time and are unable to put all your points on the final question down in the essay, write down detailed notes instead. This will at least give the examiner an idea of how much you know and should add some extra marks.

Suggested answers to tests

Page 33

Rhyming mnemonics

Possible rhyming mnemonics for the names and numbers are:

"441-0995
is for the girl inside the hive"

"255-0241
gives the boy who shines the sun"

"556-224
a thing that sticks onto the door"

"438-7468
two of these on the garden gate"

Initial letter mnemonic

The classic mnemonic for the star classification is:

"Oh be a fine girl, kiss me right now sweetheart."

Initial letter mnemonic

The classic mnemonic for the cranial nerves is:

"On old Olympia's towering top, a Finn and German vault and hop."

Rhyming mnemonics

Possible rhyming mnemonics for the dates are:

"In fifteen hundred and eighty-seven, the Queen of Scots was sent to heaven"

"In fifteen hundred and eighty-eight, the great Armada met its fate"

"In seventeen hundred and seventy-five, Washington's army came alive"

"In nineteen-hundred and thirty-three Adolf Hitler took over Germany"

Page 40

Long numbers

Possible words to link together:

Film, actor, poppy

Devil, bridge, zebra

Melon, guest, cushion

Radish, polka, stage

Bacon, purse, shirt

Giraffe, spear, lemon

Kipper, doctor, lamp

Funfair, gorilla, toffee

Jester, mountain, table

Carrot, telephone, rabbit

Appointments

Possible words to link to appointments:

Dunes	Radish
Nuts	Leather
Nature	Jeans
Map	Kids

Page 41

Historical dates

Possible words to link to events:

Canal	Robin	Thug
Kite	Lark	Door
Revel	Fairy	
Cape	Sharp	

Index